Acting Edition

To Tokyo &
The Moon

by Steve Yockey

SAMUEL FRENCH

FOR PRODUCTION INQUIRIES

UNITED STATES AND CANADA
info@concordtheatricals.com
1-866-979-0447

UNITED KINGDOM AND EUROPE
licensing@concordtheatricals.co.uk
020-7054-7298

Each title is subject to availability from Concord Theatricals Corp., depending upon country of performance. Please be aware that *TO TOKYO & THE MOON* may not be licensed by Concord Theatricals Corp. in your territory. Professional and amateur producers should contact the nearest Concord Theatricals Corp. office or licensing partner to verify availability.

No one shall make any changes in this title(s) for the purpose of production. No part of this book may be reproduced, stored in a retrieval system, scanned, uploaded, or transmitted in any form, by any means, now known or yet to be invented, including mechanical, electronic, digital, photocopying, recording, videotaping, or otherwise, without the prior written permission of the publisher. No one shall share this title(s), or any part of this title(s), through any social media or file hosting websites.

For all inquiries regarding motion picture, television, online/digital and other media rights, please contact Concord Theatricals Corp.

MUSIC AND THIRD-PARTY MATERIALS USE NOTE

Licensees are solely responsible for obtaining formal written permission from copyright owners to use copyrighted music and/or other copyrighted third-party materials (e.g. artworks, logos) in the performance of this play and are strongly cautioned to do so. If no such permission is obtained by the licensee, then the licensee must use only original music and materials that the licensee owns and controls. Licensees are solely responsible and liable for clearances of all third-party copyrighted materials, including without limitation music, and shall indemnify the copyright owners of the play(s) and their licensing agent, Concord Theatricals Corp., against any costs, expenses, losses and liabilities arising from the use of such copyrighted third-party materials by licensees. For music, please contact the appropriate music licensing authority in your territory for the rights to any incidental music.

IMPORTANT BILLING AND CREDIT REQUIREMENTS

If you have obtained performance rights to this title, please refer to your licensing agreement for important billing and credit requirements.

TO TOKYO & THE MOON was commissioned by the Kennedy Center for the Performing Arts as part of the John F. Kennedy Centennial. It premiered at the Bing Crosby Theatre in Spokane, WA, as a part of the Region VII Kennedy Center American College Theatre Festival on February 22, 2018. The production was directed by Shea King. The cast was as follows:

BEVERLY . . . . Kelly Quinnett

JANET . . . . Gail Harder

SUSAN . . . . Kameron Nichols

SAKURA . . . . Hanah Toyoda

CHORUS . . . . Dan Cassilagio, Tyson Coles, Valerie Denton,
Andrew Yoder, Cecil Milliken, Maggie Espinoza,
and Aidan Leonard

CHARACTERS

BEVERLY – A woman, sardonic, exhausted, but a picture of poise and humor in the face of epic loss.

JANET – A young woman, Beverly's older daughter, acts too hip to care, but is really struggling.

SUSAN – A young woman, Beverly's younger daughter, full of spirit, bold, and incredibly stubborn.

SAKURA – A woman, Japanese, lovely and patient, very Pierre Cardin circa 1960s, visiting the United States. She's frankly confused by her current situation but far too polite to speak up.

CHORUS – A group of people, various and sundry experts in the many aspects of astrophysics.

AUTHOR'S NOTES

[ ] in the script indicate overlapping dialogue.

The set is mid-century modern American living room with a front door that leads out into the world. Outside the front door, high above the house, a robust and lustrous full moon hangs.

Sakura's Japanese is a conversational middle ground. Casual and gentle. Contextually, she's speaking to someone she knows well.

This all moves swiftly, careening ahead. It isn't very thoughtful, especially on the front end. It shouldn't be freighted with meaning.

We choose to go to the moon. We choose to go to the moon in this decade and do the other things, not because they are easy, but because they are hard, because that goal will serve to organize and measure the best of our energies and skills, because that challenge is one that we are willing to accept, one we are unwilling to postpone, and one which we intend to win, and the others, too.

– John Fitzgerald Kennedy

1. After The Funeral

(A mid-century modern living room. There is a front door leading to a small outside area. Suburban. Above that area, a full moon hangs in the sky.)

*(***BEVERLY, JANET, SUSAN,*** and ***SAKURA*** enter. ***BEVERLY, JANET,*** and ***SUSAN*** are in all black. They look like they just came from a funeral. ***BEVERLY*** is carrying an arrangement of crisp, white flowers in a crystal vase or vessel of some kind. She can manage it with one hand or arm. ***SAKURA*** is in a chic vintage Pierre Cardin outfit from the 1960s with large, mod sunglasses and a handbag.)*

*(As ***BEVERLY*** and ***SUSAN*** take off coats, hang them up, and settle in, ***JANET*** stays near the door. ***BEVERLY*** does not put down the flower arrangement. She works around it for other tasks.)*

BEVERLY. Finally! That traffic, ugh, it's already dark out. Oh, Sakura, feel free to have a seat there on the couch. Or anywhere, I suppose.

*(***SAKURA*** just sits quietly on one end of the sofa.)*

That's perfect. Everyone, coats off. And please no throwing things [down just anywhere.]

SUSAN. [Mom, stop. You're] such a micro-manager.

BEVERLY. Honey, don't say that.

JANET. You interrupted the service multiple times to footnote people's stories [about Dad?]

SUSAN. [Like, stories] about Dad that didn't involve you.

BEVERLY. I think context is important. Janet, take that off and hang it up.

SUSAN. I'll be back in a minute!

> *(**SUSAN** runs out the front door and looks up at the moon. **JANET** just stands there. She doesn't remove her coat. But **BEVERLY** doesn't notice, her focus turned to **SAKURA**.)*

BEVERLY. Sakura, this is our home. Welcome. Would you like anything?

SAKURA. No, thank you.

BEVERLY. Well, I'm going to have a scotch neat. Janet, for God's sake, take off your coat and hang it up.

JANET. I'm not staying.

> *(**SUSAN** rushes back inside, slamming the door.)*

BEVERLY. Susan, don't slam the door.

SUSAN. I'm excited. I'm going to the moon. I've just taken a moments-long constitutional and definitively decided: I will go to the moon.

BEVERLY. Honey, no you won't. Now Janet, where exactly do you think you're off to this evening?

JANET. I'm going to [meet up with…]

SUSAN. [Mom, I'm going] to the moon. Dad used to tell me all the time I could do anything I put my mind to, even going to the moon. And that if I ever did, he'd be waiting there for me. So I'm going.

BEVERLY. Susan, your father was speaking symbolically. And even though he was an incredible man, we all know that he drank quite a bit, let's just be honest about things.

SAKURA. The moon is quite lovely.

BEVERLY. Well, I don't think anyone is disputing that.

SAKURA. But the moon is also so lonely, don't you think? It's almost like all the longing in the world has been wrapped into a ball and hung in the sky. We cannot touch it, but it waits for us to reach out. It yearns for us to try.

SUSAN. See, Sakura gets it.

BEVERLY. Sakura is our guest [and she may...]

JANET. [Mom, she] is not our guest.

BEVERLY. She is sitting right there and she can hear you. Now Sakura is welcome to share deep and moving reveries that cause all of us to reflect on our own relationships to the moon, but that does not change the fact that I'd like you to drop this business about physically going there.

SUSAN. Unfortunately, I can't because I am going to the moon.

BEVERLY. You can't go to the moon.

SUSAN. Not with that attitude.

JANET. All right, I'm leaving now.

BEVERLY. Janet, hold it right there. Susan, what I meant is that you are a young woman with no resources. Maybe one day you could go to the moon, but not anytime soon. Plus you have a clarinet recital next Tuesday and I am going to hear you play that Copland "Clarinet Concerto" excerpt.

JANET. Oh wow, I don't have to go to [that, do I?]

BEVERLY. [Yes, you have] to go, be supportive of your sister.

SUSAN. If you supported me then you would have let me play "Dream March and Circus Music" from *The Red Pony* like I wanted.

BEVERLY. Copland's "Clarinet Concerto" is a better selection.

SUSAN. They're both by Copland!

BEVERLY. Honey, I'm doing my best to keep it together today and I didn't make the rules of music. Or physics. You simply cannot be an entire orchestra. You are one clarinet. So the "Clarinet Concerto" just makes more sense.

SUSAN. You're really good at telling me all the things I can't do.

BEVERLY. Fine. But answer me this: you're going to the moon all by yourself?

SUSAN. Obviously I'm not going to do it by myself. I'm going to assemble a team of experts, various and sundry experts. I'm going to challenge them with a deadline and make it a possibility. Historically that works.

(*She rushes out of the room.* **BEVERLY** *turns to* **SAKURA**…)

BEVERLY. The imagination on this one.

(**SAKURA** *smiles and shrugs.*)

JANET. Mom, don't aside to her. She's not your ally or your confidante or whatever you imagine. She's your hostage.

BEVERLY. Don't be ridiculous. She's visiting. You're visiting from where?

SAKURA. Tokyo.

BEVERLY. How nice.

JANET. Mom.

BEVERLY. She was lost and we're going to help her.

JANET. She was not lost. You kept asking, "Are you lost?" over and over again while leading her away from the cemetery and putting her into our car and bringing her back to our house.

BEVERLY. Now, honey, that is a massive oversimplification.

SAKURA. I hoped to see the eternal flame.

JANET. See? She's just too polite to tell you this is false imprisonment.

BEVERLY. Well, we will help Sakura get to the eternal flame. In the meantime, I'm reading a biography on Kennedy and we can compare notes. Honestly, thank goodness we came along when we did or who knows how long you may have been lost?

JANET. Mom, you've taken her literally miles from where [she wants to be.]

BEVERLY. [You know it pains] me to say this, but you have never understood charitable behavior or simple kindness, Janet. Honestly, I blame myself.

JANET. I blame you, too. For kidnapping a tourist.

BEVERLY. I understand you are upset about your father's death. But channeling your rage towards me isn't going to make things better.

JANET. Oh. Okay. And I understand that you feel powerless to fix that he's gone, and it breaks my heart. But channeling those feelings into abducting a woman to fix a problem that you created in order to have purpose and feel agency in the world is not going to make things better either.

BEVERLY. Well let me just rush outside and check the mailbox to see if our degrees in advanced psychoanalysis have arrived yet!

(**SUSAN** *rushes back on with an enormous, old school phone book.*)

SUSAN. Dad said I could go to the moon and I'm going to prove him right!

> *(She rushes over to a nearby table, pulls the TouchTone crimp-corded phone over, sets down the giant phone book, and starts searching for numbers. Eventually she starts making calls and having muffled conversations about going to the moon.)*

BEVERLY. Well, I can't stop you, so go ahead. Be bold, Susan. Just please clean up after yourself. Janet, if you're done hating everything would you please fix Sakura some tea?

JANET. I can call the police for her?

BEVERLY. Janet, I'm so exhausted.

JANET. I can't make her tea. I'm leaving. I'm going to meet up with Evan.

BEVERLY. You most certainly are not going to meet up with Evan.

JANET. You wouldn't let him come to the funeral and now you won't even let me see him? What kind of a police state is this?

BEVERLY. It's the kind of police state where your new boyfriend with all of those charming tattoos can wait while you stay here to eat [with your family.]

JANET. [Ugh, I don't want] any of this "sad people" food. Everyone keeps bringing us "sad people" food.

BEVERLY. It now seems clear you are not done hating everything yet.

JANET. Like how many green bean casseroles can one family eat?

BEVERLY. It's because the recipe is on the can.

JANET. And that stupid peach pie, did you taste that stupid peach pie?

BEVERLY. Not yet. Honey, people don't know what to do when someone dies. They feel awkward. So they bring food. It's comforting. Anyway, it's supposed to be comforting. At least it feels like an effort.

JANET. Those peaches don't taste like someone cared. They taste like they came from a can. They taste. Like they came. From a can.

BEVERLY. Don't be a snob.

JANET. I'm not eating it.

BEVERLY. Be brave, Janet.

JANET. I'm not eating any of it.

BEVERLY. Then it will all go to waste! What good does that do? Honestly, what on earth has you in such a mood today?

JANET. Dad is dead!

SUSAN. Hey! Keep it down! I'm on the phone with various and sundry experts.

> (**JANET** *crosses her arms and slumps into a chair in a huff. Pause.* **BEVERLY** *crosses over and kneels next to her.*)

BEVERLY. Today is a very difficult day. The service was difficult. And the truth of it will hit us in wave after wave. We must brace ourselves. We must brace each other.

> (*Pause.*)

JANET. I'm sorry I yelled.

BEVERLY. That's all right. I'm not sure there are any rules about days like today.

JANET. Mom?

BEVERLY. Yes, honey?

JANET. You don't like Evan, do you?

BEVERLY. Clearly not.

JANET. Mom?

BEVERLY. Yes?

JANET. Are you going to put down that flower arrangement?

BEVERLY. Eventually.

> (**SUSAN** *hangs up the phone and makes an announcement.*)

SUSAN. You'll be happy to know that everything is coming together. Beautifully. Thank you for your begrudging support family! I will remember you fondly in the wake of my grand success.

> (*She takes the phone book and marches off.*)

JANET. Mom, I think something's very wrong with Susan.

BEVERLY. She's just upset. But honestly, honey, it's good for her to dream. Dreams are especially important during bleak times. We need...we need things to hold on to in the dark. Now, let's go eat some of that "sad food," all right? I'll try a slice of that peach pie you hate so much.

> (**JANET** *and* **BEVERLY** *head into the kitchen.* **BEVERLY** *does not put down the flower arrangement.*)

> (*They've all left* **SAKURA** *sitting alone. She takes off her sunglasses. The lights dim as a warm special rises on her. She reaches into her purse and takes out her smartphone. She dials and waits. As* **SAKURA** *speaks, an English translation of her words appears in supertitles somewhere else onstage.*)

SAKURA. Konnichiwa.

Uun. Heiki heiki. Shinpai sasete gomenne.

Jitsuwa, ima doko ni iru no wa wakaranaikedo.

Shiranai kazoku ni yuukaisarete shimatta.

Uun, kikendewa nai to omouyo. Ocha demo kuretashi.

Sugoku kanashii kazoku shika mienaiwa.

Itsumade kenkinsareru no wa mada wakaranaikedo.

Dameyo, shitsurei to omowanai?

Ah, souda, kurerunetto no konsaato ni derukamo shirenai yo.

Un, doumo. Mada denwa kakeruwa.

Otsukare.

[Hello.

No. I'm fine, I'm fine. I am sorry to have worried you.

Actually, I don't really know where I am right now.

I am abducted by a family that I don't know.

No, I don't think they are dangerous. They even gave me tea.

They only seem like a very sad family.

I don't know until when I will be held hostage.

No. That's rude, don't you think?

Oh, right, I might be attending a clarinet concert.

Yes, thank you. I will call you again.

Take care.]

(She hangs up the phone as the lights fade out.)

2. One Week Later

(It is one week later. **BEVERLY**, **SUSAN**, *and* **SAKURA** *are having tea in the living room.* **SAKURA** *is basically in the exact same place.* **SUSAN** *is taking apart her clarinet and putting it away. She has a pile of rolled-up blueprints and a hardhat sitting beside her on the couch.* **BEVERLY** *is still holding the flower arrangement. And it is still crisp and white.)*

BEVERLY. What a nice evening. It was a wonderful recital.

SUSAN. Thank you. Thank you for coming, Sakura.

(**SAKURA** *smiles and shrugs.)*

BEVERLY. I feel you were the strongest performer, in my [humble opinion.]

SUSAN. [Mom, it's not a] contest.

BEVERLY. I know, honey. But all the same, you were the best. And your father would have been proud.

SUSAN. I'm glad. But the music from *The Red Pony* would have been better.

BEVERLY. No one even remembers that movie.

SUSAN. As long as you're happy.

(She closes her clarinet case, shoves it under the couch, drinks her tea in one gulp, then gets up and begins to collect her blueprints.)

BEVERLY. Don't you want to sit with us?

SUSAN. Listen, I have respectfully scheduled my moon mission around this recital because it was important to you. And you were unwilling to postpone.

BEVERLY. It was a challenge to be faced boldly, not pushed into the future.

SUSAN. You're right. But it's done now, you're pleased, and I have various and sundry experts scheduled to be here tonight. Plus, Dad is waiting. So thank you, I'm glad you had a nice time, and I'm going to work.

SAKURA. The moon is so full tonight. Did you notice? You can feel the [pull of its...]

BEVERLY. [Yes, yes, it's] lonely and unrequited. Thank you. Susan, if you're going outside then take a jacket.

SUSAN. Fine.

> *(She has her blueprints and hardhat, but she manages to pull a jacket off the coatrack. She exits the house into the front area. While the conversation inside continues, she puts on her jacket and her hardhat and waits.)*

BEVERLY. I didn't mean to interrupt you just then. I was just worried that she would go outside without her coat. Wouldn't that be a disaster?

SAKURA. Perhaps.

BEVERLY. It is quite chilly and only getting colder.

SAKURA. Perhaps.

BEVERLY. You know, it occurs to me that we were supposed to get you to the eternal flame. I suppose that was a week ago now? Ultimately, it is a testament to how well you fit in here, don't you think?

SAKURA. Perhaps.

BEVERLY. I almost said it with you that time so we could say "jinx." Isn't that fun? Do you know that game? Probably not.

> *(Outside, a **CHORUS** of various and sundry experts arrives to meet with **SUSAN**. Men. Women. Some in hardhats. Some with blueprints. Shirts and ties, skirts and blouses, all business. They begin a conversation. They point at the blueprints. They point at the moon.)*

SAKURA. Beverly, it is amazing how those flowers have maintained their robust health since the funeral service. They are still so crisp and white.

BEVERLY. Well, the service isn't officially over until I put them down. So congratulations to these flowers for doing their job admirably.

SAKURA. When do you think you might set them aside?

BEVERLY. I don't know.

SAKURA. Mmhm.

BEVERLY. You know we don't have to keep dry-cleaning that one outfit. You are more than welcome to borrow some of my clothes while you're visiting.

SAKURA. I am fine, thank you.

> *(**JANET** pushes past **SUSAN** and the **CHORUS** outside and storms into the house. She might not be crying now, but she's been crying recently. She's demonstrably upset.)*

JANET. Who are, who are all those people out front?

BEVERLY. Where have you been? You missed your sister's gorgeous recital.

JANET. Lucky me!

BEVERLY. You promised to be there, young lady.

JANET. That's a lie.

BEVERLY. Janet!

JANET. Evan broke up with me!! He says my hair isn't as shiny and I'm still too sad about Dad dying and it's making me a bummer to be around, but I think he really just found another girl who is less generally depressing.

BEVERLY. Either way, he sounds like a terrible person. He's a terrible person. They can't all be winners. Trust me. Sometimes you make a poor choice and as it dawns on you the disappointment is compounded.

JANET. But I still choose him.

BEVERLY. You'll come to your senses.

JANET. No! I want to be the girl he wants me to be, happy, carefree, afraid her dad might catch her sneaking into the house, which he can't do because he's in a box in the ground forever.

(She begins to cry.)

(Outside the front door, **SUSAN** *leads the* **CHORUS** *offstage.)*

BEVERLY. Honey, sit down.

*(***JANET** *doesn't move.)*

All right, stand. Standing is fine; it helps the circulation. Now of course you want to be that girl. And you will be happy, and hopefully as carefree as anyone ever can be, but your father is gone.

JANET. I know.

BEVERLY. And all the rest of it just makes you human. Things like desire, regret, confusion, a need to feel validated. Which reminds me, I don't want to say I told you so, but I absolutely did tell he was trouble.

SAKURA. Beverly.

BEVERLY. Well, I did. If she had just listened to me [in the first place...]

JANET. [Congratulations! You] were right and now I just want to end my life!

BEVERLY. Honey, there will be other boys. Don't threaten to kill yourself in front of our guest. She might not know you're just being dramatic.

JANET. She's been here for a week. She knows. She's just too polite to say you're still keeping her prisoner and that I'm completely insane. But she knows.

SAKURA. I do know.

BEVERLY. First of all, no one expects you to "get over" the death of your father in a few weeks. Except perhaps that terrible, thoughtless, tattooed boy. You'll grieve in your own time and in your own way and you'll discover for yourself what it means to keep going. No one can do that for you: no person, no book, no radio program, etc. You're the only one.

JANET. Okay.

> (**SUSAN** *leads the* **CHORUS** *back on. As a group, they carry an immense ladder. When they stand it up, it reaches the moon hanging above the set. Everyone is very pleased, shaking hands and smiling.)*

BEVERLY. And break-ups happen. We have to handle them with a certain amount of class. Yes. We must be classy.

JANET. God, Mom, there's no classy way to handle this.

BEVERLY. By "classy" I really just mean graceful and self-possessed. And please know for the rest of your life that, barring torture, there is most likely a graceful, classy way to handle almost anything.

JANET. Like what's an example? That doesn't have to do with being abandoned by the love of your life?

BEVERLY. The love of your life? Oh no. You're so prone to hyperbole, Janet. It's remarkable. Did you hear her, Sakura? The love of her life.

(**SAKURA** *smiles and shrugs.*)

JANET. I told you to stop asiding to Sakura, now just give me an example.

BEVERLY. All right. Hmm. Oh, all right! Let's say, for instance, if you were serving in the navy [and your boat…]

JANET. [Ugh, I can't handle] any more from that Kennedy biography, Mom.

BEVERLY. Now, honey. Just because I said navy "doesn't" [mean that…]

JANET. [Is this from] the Kennedy biography?

BEVERLY. Yes.

JANET. Ugh, I want to find whoever gave it to you after the funeral and punch them right in the face.

BEVERLY. This violent streak.

JANET. Can't you just give me an example from real [life that's…]

BEVERLY. [Now hold on, this] will be very applicable. Let me get to it.

JANET. Fine.

BEVERLY. Good. Now, for instance, let's say some people happened to destroy the naval boat you were serving on and you spent days at sea with your crew. Somehow you survived, but most of your friends did not. With me so far?

JANET. Mom, this is really tragic.

BEVERLY. Yes. But then Janet, then much later, when given the opportunity to be in charge, you put away any resentments towards those people that destroyed your boat, you put away your personal grudges, and reached out to heal that relationship. For the greater good of everyone. That's an example of handling a difficult situation with class. Right, Sakura?

SAKURA. Yes.

BEVERLY. Yes.

SAKURA. After those people who destroyed the boat recovered from a terrifying, unprecedented, and traumatizing nuclear winter. Yes.

(*Pause.*)

BEVERLY. Okay, well, that example is perhaps more complicated than I intended. Or requires more nuance. But then, that in and of itself is a very important life lesson. Things can be messy and complex and unfair and you have to stay strong in spite of them, in the face of them.

> (*After some discussion,* **SUSAN** *begins to climb the ladder. She has a megaphone on a strap over her shoulder, a small cooler probably also over her shoulder, and a bottle of water.*)

JANET. I just want Evan back.

BEVERLY. I don't think that's what's best for you. But ultimately, you have no control over what this terrible boy wants, so you have to let him go.

JANET. You know, if I'm being honest, I don't really want him back. I just want to be wanted. I would... I want to feel classy and be wanted.

BEVERLY. Oh, honey, you and everyone else in the whole wide world.

*(She hugs **JANET** with her free arm. **JANET** hugs her back. **SAKURA** removes her sunglasses and uses a handkerchief from her purse to dab tears from her eyes.)*

*(At the same time, **SUSAN** reaches the moon and sits on top of it. The **CHORUS** cheers and applauds.)*

JANET. You never told me, who are all of those people on the front lawn?

BEVERLY. I have no idea, but they're certainly excited about something.

*(**BEVERLY** and **JANET** go to the door and open it.)*

CHORUS. Congratulations!

JANET. Congratulations on what?

BEVERLY. Excuse me, but you're standing on my perennials.

CHORUS. Susan has gone to the moon!

BEVERLY. No, she hasn't.

CHORUS. Yes, she has.

BEVERLY. Don't be ridiculous!

CHORUS. With the help of this dedicated and passionate team of various and sundry experts, Susan has successfully gone to the moon!

*(They all point to the moon. **SUSAN** is there.)*

BEVERLY. Oh my god.

JANET. Mom, she did it.

BEVERLY. Oh my god!

JANET. She actually did it!

BEVERLY. You come down from the moon right now, young lady!

> (**SUSAN** *clicks on the megaphone and speaks through it.*)

SUSAN. Hello family. With very little nurturing or support from you I have achieved the first part of my dream of going to the moon. Please give these hardworking various and sundry experts a late supper to thank them on my behalf, as I have taken all of the Capri-Sun and string cheese for my journey. Now I will go to look for Dad. Please take my clarinet in for a tune up at the instrument shop if I'm not back in a month. Farewell!

> (**SUSAN** *disappears behind the moon.*)

BEVERLY. Susan? Susan! Susan!!

JANET. Mom, what are we going to do now? Susan is on the moon, she's really [on the moon!]

BEVERLY. [Don't panic! We're] going to call NASA. Is that right? We're going to call the government and NASA and anyone else we can think of and we're going to do it right now.

CHORUS. What about supper?

BEVERLY. What about supper?

CHORUS. Susan said we could have a late supper?

JANET. Are you serious? What if she's in trouble?

CHORUS. She's fine.

JANET. You sent a girl to the moon and now you want food?!

CHORUS. We're hungry.

JANET. Tough.

CHORUS. Hey! This was hard work, okay?

BEVERLY. Janet, they're right. You're right.

CHORUS. Okay then.

BEVERLY. You're right and Susan is safe for the moment, relatively safe within the context of solo space exploration?

CHORUS. We're good at our jobs.

BEVERLY. All right. Then I'll try not to let my anxiety attack about the fate of my youngest daughter get in the way of rewarding your clearly Herculean accomplishment.

CHORUS. Sounds great.

BEVERLY. Follow me to the kitchen. We'll make you a late supper and then we'll call everyone.

> *(She and **JANET** move with purpose through the front door, across the living room, and into the kitchen. The entire **CHORUS** of various and sundry experts follows them.)*

> *(They've all left **SAKURA** sitting alone. Again. The lights dim as a warm special rises on her. She reaches into her purse, puts away her handkerchief, and takes out her smartphone. She dials and waits. As **SAKURA** speaks, an English translation of her words appears in supertitles somewhere else onstage.)*

SAKURA. Konnichiwa.

Souyone, hondoni hisashiburiyone. Minna genki?

Yokkata.

Un, zannenkedo itsu modoreru no wa mada wakaranai.

Ichiban shita no musume-san tsukini ittanode koko no minnasan sugoku shinpai shiteru sou. Sonna ni taihen na jiki ni gomeiwaku kaketakunai yo.

Aitai. Mada denwa kakeru wa.

Otsukare.

[Hello.

Yes. It has been a long time. How's the family?

That's good.

Yes. Unfortunately, I don't know when I will be returning.

The youngest daughter went to the moon and the family seems to be worried about it. I don't want to be a bother during such a stressful time.

I want to see you. I will contact you again.

Take care.]

> *(She hangs up the phone as the lights fade out.)*

3. Some Time Later

*(It is some time later. It is night. **SAKURA** is sitting on the couch in basically the same place. Folded up sheets and a pillow are stacked by her side on the couch. A lamp sitting next to her provides the only light. She is reading Beverly's copy of the JFK biography.)*

*(The **CHORUS** of various and sundry experts are asleep on the ground outside the door.)*

*(**SUSAN** is still on the moon.)*

*(**BEVERLY** enters in some kind of nightgown and robe. She is carrying the flower arrangement. It is still crisp, white, and full.)*

BEVERLY. Oh, Sakura. You're awake.

SAKURA. I am reading this biography you left on the credenza.

BEVERLY. Oh! Oh, it's such a good book, isn't it? Well, don't let me interrupt. I'm going to get some warm milk. I find it helps me sleep.

SAKURA. Hmmm.

BEVERLY. Because I'm having trouble sleeping. It's actually quite vexing.

SAKURA. Would you like to sit?

BEVERLY. Oh, I don't mean to disturb you.

*(**BEVERLY** sits with **SAKURA** on the couch anyway.)*

SAKURA. You are worried for your youngest daughter.

BEVERLY. I'm worried for both my daughters. But yes, my immediate concern is for my youngest daughter, Susan. The one on the moon.

SAKURA. It's romantic isn't it? Not "love" romantic, but more lovely and idealistic.

BEVERLY. It's a rock with no atmosphere.

SAKURA. Some people believe the moon and sun were married once and are now separated forever. Now the moon chases the sun around the Earth, but never catches sight. There is something of an ache to it, don't you agree?

BEVERLY. Well, it is terrible to be separated from your loved one.

   (**SAKURA** *looks absentmindedly at the wedding ring on her finger.*)

SAKURA. Yes.

BEVERLY. But I have to tell myself that it's not forever.

SAKURA. I believe Susan will be back. She has ingenuity and spirit. She is a remarkable young lady to have accomplished such a feat.

BEVERLY. There is a difference between being remarkable and being thoughtful.

SAKURA. That's very true.

BEVERLY. I just have to trust in these various and sundry experts.

SAKURA. And trust in Susan. And trust in yourself. You are strong. I have seen you with your daughters, witnessed your life. Honestly, I don't have much else to do.

BEVERLY. We need to get you a hobby.

   (**SAKURA** *takes* **BEVERLY**'*s hand.*)

SAKURA. Beverly, I believe you are quite capable of handling any hardships life may send your way. If you let yourself. In the same way that I know I can handle the unexpected turns that life throws at me. With as much, what was the word you used? "Grace?" Yes, we can be graceful and classy.

BEVERLY. How unexpected, I appreciate that. But it isn't really about me now, is it? It's about my daughters. It has to be.

SAKURA. If you'd like to leave the flowers with me, I can look after them for you?

BEVERLY. Sakura.

SAKURA. Beverly.

BEVERLY. Sakura.

SAKURA. Beverly.

(Pause. And there's an ocean of unsaid things in this pause between these women.)

*(**BEVERLY** gets up to exit. She still has the flowers.)*

BEVERLY. You know, I lied to you earlier. The warm milk doesn't really help me sleep. It's a thing I believe, but it doesn't do anything. I suppose it's an empty gesture.

SAKURA. You are a remarkable woman, Beverly.

BEVERLY. Oh. Thank you. I think. Sleep well.

SAKURA. Goodnight.

*(**BEVERLY** leaves. **SAKURA** shakes her head in frustration and returns to reading the book.)*

*(Meanwhile, on the moon, **SUSAN** comes into view.)*

SUSAN. Dear Dad. You promised you'd be here. More times than I can remember. You leaned in to kiss me goodnight after reading me a story, just a hint of Bourbon on your breath because Bourbon on the rocks is a gentleman's drink, and you told me I could do anything. Even go to the moon. And if I ever did, you'd be here. But I've looked everywhere and, well, I guess you didn't make it. I'm not holding it against you or anything. I'm not cross. It's pretty barren up here and I've been lonely, especially since none of the various and sundry experts who passionately dedicated themselves to my cause could come with me. So I've had a lot to time to think and I wanted to tell you I've realized two things. First, Mom was right about the Copland "Clarinet Concerto." Second, maybe when you told me you would be here on the moon you were speaking metaphysically. Maybe great people who come before us are always there in our achievements because we never would have achieved without them in the first place. We rise on their faith and dedication. So in a sense, you are here. And you'll always be with me. Isn't that comforting? Or maybe you were just drunk. Either way, I'm heading home now so I wanted to say... Goodbye.

> *(***SUSAN*** *climbs down from the moon. She makes her way through the sleeping* **CHORUS** *of various and sundry experts, careful not to wake them, and slips through the front door into the house.)*

SAKURA. Welcome home.

SUSAN. Hello, Sakura. You're still here? I feel like I was gone for a long time.

SAKURA. You were.

SUSAN. Is it very late?

SAKURA. Yes. People need their rest.

SUSAN. All right.

(**SUSAN** *takes the megaphone strapped over her shoulder and shouts into it!*)

Family! Please join me in the living room for an announcement about my return from the moon and momentous personal growth!

SAKURA. That was very loud.

SUSAN. Thank you.

(**JANET** *rushes into the living room in a plaid "hip girl" version of men's pajamas.* **BEVERLY** *rushes in from the kitchen and turns on the lights. She is still in her nightgown and still carrying the flower arrangement. It is still crisp, white, and full.*)

JANET. Susan!

BEVERLY. Susan, you're back!

(**BEVERLY** *rushes to* **SUSAN** *and hugs her. The* **CHORUS** *of various and sundry experts outside begins to wake.*)

JANET. Why are you using that thing in the house?

SUSAN. I didn't want to wait until morning to tell you I was back in case you were having unsettled, fitful dreams about my fate. Also, I like very much to make an entrance.

(*The* **CHORUS** *notices* **SUSAN** *is not on the moon.*)

CHORUS. She's gone! Did she come back from the moon?

(*They rush to the front door and knock.* **BEVERLY** *answers.*)

BEVERLY. Yes?

CHORUS. Did Susan come back from the moon?

SUSAN. Yes, I did!

BEVERLY. Yes, she did.

CHORUS. We have various and sundry things to ask her.

SUSAN. Ask away!

BEVERLY. Now just wait, just hold on a moment. Susan will be happy to meet with you tomorrow morning. It's very late and she needs her sleep.

CHORUS. Just one question?

SUSAN. Please, Mom.

BEVERLY. Fine. Go ahead.

CHORUS. Did you find your dad?

*(Pause. Everyone looks at **SUSAN**.)*

SUSAN. I found him metaphysically and I told him goodbye.

*(**BEVERLY** tears up. But she pushes through it and wraps things up with the various and sundry experts.)*

BEVERLY. Okay, the rest can wait until the morning. Have a lovely night.

CHORUS. All right. There's also the matter of our compensation now that the mission is complete. We can discuss that tomorrow.

BEVERLY. Compensation?

CHORUS. Susan has the details. Goodnight. And welcome back, Susan! You have a lot to be proud of this evening.

SUSAN. Thank you!

*(**BEVERLY** closes the door.)*

JANET. So you...you didn't find Dad?

(**SUSAN** *crosses to* **JANET** *and takes her hands. They share a tender moment.*)

SUSAN. Janet. Dad passed away. He's gone.

JANET. I know. I just... I don't like it. And I miss him.

SUSAN. Janet. It's okay to be sad about it for as long as you need to be sad.

JANET. Thank you. I wish certain terrible boys felt the same way.

SUSAN. Janet. Dad would have hated Evan.

JANET. You're right.

(**SUSAN** *releases* **JANET**'s *hands.*)

BEVERLY. Well, that's refreshing. You girls really are something. And that's enough talk about Evan. Terrible boys are labeled terrible for a reason.

SUSAN. Because they're terrible.

BEVERLY. Yes, honey.

SUSAN. I feel like I am really knocking it out of the park on identifying truths about the human condition lately.

JANET. But what are we going to do about all of your various and sundry experts? We can't pay them with self-actualization. Wait, can we?

BEVERLY. No, honey.

SUSAN. Most of them were working from a place of raw passion, but honestly I did tell them there would be a stipend upon completion of the mission. And I'm back so technically the mission is now completed.

BEVERLY. What kind of stipend?

SUSAN. We didn't really discuss numbers. It's maybe more than a dollar but less than the cost of new, midsize car.

BEVERLY. Well, we may have to tighten our belts, but we will handle it.

JANET. Tighten our belts?

BEVERLY. Be brave, Janet.

JANET. It's funny how you always say that kind of thing about everyday problems. "Be bold, Susan." "Be brave, Janet." Like that fixes anything.

BEVERLY. Honey, courage isn't about the big things. It's about being brave during those tiny moments when it's just us and no else one is watching. It's the little choices that make us who we are when we go sleep at night.

SAKURA. When we're alone with ourselves.

BEVERLY. Yes.

SAKURA. Yes.

SUSAN. Like when I was on the moon.

SAKURA. Mmhm.

BEVERLY. This is off topic, but I just need to ask: Sakura, I thought you had just been impeccably folding the sheets every morning. But tonight I'm realizing, are you not using them to sleep on?

SAKURA. No.

BEVERLY. But they are for your comfort.

SAKURA. I am fine. I do not wish to be an imposition.

JANET. Sakura, would you like to go home?

BEVERLY. Janet, don't be rude. She is welcome to stay as long as she likes.

JANET. Be brave, Beverly.

SUSAN. Well, while you two bicker, I already have everything figured out. I'm smart and accomplished in both the clarinet and space travel. You told me to be bold and I was bold. I worked hard and it paid off.

BEVERLY. That may be true, Susan. It's not very humble, but it may be true. That said, it never hurts to be reminded. Brave and bold in every little thing.

SUSAN. Eh, it's a pretty simple equation. Dedication and curiosity equal accomplishment. I mean, I'm surprised you two don't have it down yet.

BEVERLY. Honey, I'm very proud of you. But now let me tell you the sad, grown-up truth. We all have to learn these lessons over and over again: how to be courageous, how to be strong, how to be inquisitive, how to work together, how to listen to each other, how to go to the moon. And for a moment, we are our best selves. And then the knowledge fades away. So we get to work figuring it all out again.

SUSAN. That seems unnecessarily difficult.

BEVERLY. It is.

SUSAN. And wearisome.

BEVERLY. That too.

SAKURA. But worthwhile.

BEVERLY. Absolutely.

JANET. I probably need to spend more time focused on learning those big life lessons and less time fixated in an unhealthy way on Evan.

BEVERLY. [Yes.]

SUSAN. [Yes.]

SAKURA. [Yes.]

JANET. It's occurring to me, honestly, how much time I could be spending enriching my soul. Instead of just throwing it away calling Evan, following Evan, photographing Evan, and ultimately threatening Evan.

SUSAN. I believe the umbrella term for all that is "stalking."

JANET. Probably. But looking back over the past few weeks, I can see now that those were all poor choices.

BEVERLY. Oh. Okay, good. Honey, we should talk more later about some of what you just said, but it's a good realization.

(**SUSAN** *crosses to* **JANET** *and nods towards* **BEVERLY**.)

SUSAN. We're all having realizations.

(**JANET** *nods "yes."*)

JANET. We are all having realizations. And... I know you can make brave choices, too. Mom. Brave, bold choices.

BEVERLY. Well, thank you.

SUSAN. Like you said, like learning something all over again. Or maybe like learning something for the first time, which is probably a lot scarier.

BEVERLY. Wise words.

JANET. Like learning to let things go.

(**BEVERLY** *realizes where* **JANET** *is heading and quickly deflects.*)

BEVERLY. Food for thought. Now, let's focus on getting your sister's various and sundry experts taken care of because that is the [most pressing...]

JANET. [Mom, put down] the flowers.

SUSAN. You have to put down the flowers.

BEVERLY. When you girls grow up, perhaps you'll understand more clearly. I'm not, I am just not ready to let him, I'm not ready to let them go yet. But I'll do it later; I promise I'll do it later. Trust me, any day [now I'll be...]

SUSAN. [You sat right] there and told me, "Challenges should be faced boldly, not pushed into the future."

SAKURA. I remember that.

BEVERLY. Honey, I was just paraphrasing something I read once.

JANET. Mom, if Susan went to the moon, then you can put down the flowers.

SUSAN. We can consult my various and sundry experts on the best way to put them down, the mechanics of it. Would that help?

BEVERLY. Honey, I can't.

SAKURA. Beverly. You can. You don't have to be the moon.

(Pause. **BEVERLY** *looks terrified, but she slowly puts down the flowers. Suddenly, the sound of a gust of wind and a sprinkling of chimes sweeps across the stage as hundreds or thousands of white flower petals float down from above, covering everything in the living room. It is a gorgeous blizzard of flowers.)*

*(***BEVERLY*** cries. She does not weep, she cries with a smile. She may even laugh. It is the release of acceptance.)*

(The **GIRLS** *move to her, hugging her.)*

BEVERLY. He's really gone.

JANET. I'm proud of you.

SUSAN. Me too.

(The **WOMEN** *keep hugging.* **SAKURA** *nods knowingly, collects her things, gets up, and heads for the front door.)*

BEVERLY. Oh, Sakura. You're not you leaving, are you? We'll have a nice dinner and then tomorrow morning we can finally take you to see the eternal flame. Wouldn't want you getting lost in the meantime.

SAKURA. That...that sounds lovely.

(**SAKURA** *smiles and shrugs. She moves back to the couch and sits.*)

SUSAN. Oh! We should have macaroni & cheese for dinner.

BEVERLY. It was your father's favorite.

SUSAN. And also hot dogs, green beans, mashed potatoes, pork chops, baked beans, those weird deviled eggs, maybe some waffles, oh, fried chicken, cantaloupe, [definitely sweet tea...]

JANET. [Whoa, whoa, Susan,] you can eat all that?

SUSAN. I mean, I haven't had anything but Capri-Sun and string cheese for a really long time. So yes I can.

JANET. How did you breathe up there?

SUSAN. Carefully.

BEVERLY. Well, Susan, we can't eat all of that because it would kill us. But we can have selections from your staggering list. I'll prepare the food.

SUSAN. And I can tell you all about what I did on the moon.

JANET. And I can tell you all about what I did to Evan's car before I recently became more enlightened and focused on my future.

(*The* **WOMEN** *move into the kitchen. Together. A family.*)

(*Surprising no one, they have left* **SAKURA** *alone again. The lights dim as a warm special rises on her. She sighs, reaches into*

*her purse and takes out her smartphone. She
dials and waits.)*

SAKURA. Konnichiwa...

[Hello...]

(Blackout.)

End of Play

www.ingramcontent.com/pod-product-compliance
Lightning Source LLC
Chambersburg PA
CBHW070422120726
47909CB00005B/1755